Flicka, Ricka, Dicka
BAKE A CAKE
MAJ LINDMAN

ALBERT WHITMAN & COMPANY
Morton Grove, Illinois

The Snipp, Snapp, Snurr Books
Snipp, Snapp, Snurr and the Buttered Bread
Snipp, Snapp, Snurr and the Gingerbread
Snipp, Snapp, Snurr and the Red Shoes
Snipp, Snapp, Snurr Learn to Swim

The Flicka, Ricka, Dicka Books
Flicka, Ricka, Dicka and the Little Dog
Flicka, Ricka, Dicka and the New Dotted Dresses
Flicka, Ricka, Dicka and the Three Kittens
Flicka, Ricka, Dicka Bake a Cake

Library of Congress Cataloging-in-Publication Data
Lindman, Maj.
Flicka, Ricka, Dicka bake a cake / Maj Lindman.
p.   cm.
Summary: Three little Swedish sisters bake two cakes for
their mother's birthday surprise, one a burned catastrophe,
but the second a golden success.
ISBN 0-8075-2480-8
[1. Baking—Fiction. 2. Sisters—Fiction. 3. Sweden—Fiction.] I. Title.
PZ7.L659Fn 1995   94-37261
[Fic]—dc20   CIP
                                              AC

The text is set in 23' Futura Book
and 12' Bookman Light Italic.

A Flicka, Ricka, Dicka Book

One afternoon the three girls went to visit Aunt Betty.

Flicka, Ricka, and Dicka were three sisters who lived in Sweden. They had blue eyes and yellow curls.

Aunt Betty lived near the girls.

She was not really their aunt. But they had called her Aunt Betty since they first began to talk. Aunt Betty had also cared for Mother when she was a little girl.

One afternoon the three girls went to visit Aunt Betty. As they sat on the floor beside her, Flicka said, "Aunt Betty, what can we give Mother for her birthday tomorrow?"

Ricka said, "Father thinks that Mother would like something we might make. What should it be?"

Aunt Betty thought a moment. Then she said, "Why don't you bake her a birthday cake?"

"But we don't know how to bake a cake!" exclaimed Flicka.

"Aunt Betty does," said Ricka. "She can show us how."

"Will you please, Aunt Betty?" asked Dicka.

"Of course I will," she said. "I've made many cakes for your mother. I know which ones she likes."

She went to get two cookbooks. The three little girls watched her look through them.

The three little girls watched her look through them.

Here is what I am looking for," Aunt Betty said. "I remember this is the cake she always liked best. Flicka, make a list of these things: flour, sugar, butter, eggs, raisins, cream, baking powder."

"We'll hurry to the grocery store and get all we need," said Ricka.

Aunt Betty nodded as she handed Dicka a market basket.

The three girls hurried to the grocery store at the corner. Flicka gave the list to a man with red hair.

He held up a box in his right hand. "Here's the box of raisins," he said.

"Here's the box of raisins," he said.

He put the groceries into the basket and handed it to Ricka and Dicka.

Soon the girls were back in Aunt Betty's kitchen. She gave them striped aprons to wear. A large blue bowl, a wooden spoon, and a cake pan were ready on the table.

Aunt Betty said, "First, you mix the butter and sugar. Next, you beat the eggs. Add the beaten eggs and cream to the butter and sugar and mix some more. Now, mix the baking powder and flour; add both to the batter. Flicka, don't forget to put in the raisins."

Flicka stirred all these things in the large blue bowl.

Dicka put wood into the stove.

Ricka buttered the cake pan.

Dicka put wood into the stove.

When everything in the bowl was smooth and yellow, Flicka poured it into the cake pan.

"The oven is hot now," said Dicka as she opened the oven door.

Flicka carried the cake pan to the stove. She put it into the oven and closed the door tightly.

"It is five minutes after twelve," said Aunt Betty. "The cake should bake for about half an hour. I am going out for awhile. When you have cleaned up the dishes, why don't you all go outside to cool off?

"But remember—your cake should bake just half an hour."

All three little girls washed the dishes and put them away.

Flicka carried the cake pan to the stove.

After they had wiped the kitchen table, they ran into the garden. They took off their striped aprons because they were very warm.

Dicka saw a piece of rope on the kitchen porch. Soon the three girls were jumping rope.

They sang little songs as they jumped up and down. Then they all shouted together, "Sugar—pepper—salt—mustard—vinegar!" With each word they turned the rope faster and faster.

The girl who was jumping hopped faster and faster, too.

Suddenly Flicka cried, "Oh, my! The cake!"

Soon the three girls were jumping rope.

Flicka, Ricka, and Dicka ran to the kitchen. Heavy gray smoke was pouring out of the oven.

"It's nearly one-fifteen!" cried Flicka as she looked at the clock on the wall.

"Our cake must be burning!" said Ricka.

Flicka opened the oven door. More smoke poured out. "What a bad smell!" she cried.

"Aunt Betty told us the cake should bake just half an hour," Ricka said.

"Oh," said Dicka sadly. "Why did we forget Mother's birthday cake? We shouldn't have played so long."

Heavy gray smoke was pouring out of the oven.

When Flicka had found a big towel, she took the hot cake pan out of the oven. She carried it to the middle of the kitchen and stood looking at it.

"The cake's as black as ink!" cried Ricka.

"It's all burned up," agreed Flicka.

"It isn't fit to eat," Dicka added. "Why didn't we watch the clock as Aunt Betty said?" Big tears rolled down her face.

"We were so busy having fun we forgot about it," said Flicka.

Just then Aunt Betty came home.

They all stood looking at the cake.

It's too bad," she said when they told her what had happened. "But crying won't help now. We'll just have to bake another cake. You will find it much easier to do the second time."

Soon the butter, sugar, eggs, flour, baking powder, cream, and raisins were all mixed together again in the big blue bowl.

Each little girl took her turn at stirring.

Aunt Betty put more wood into the stove. Then she washed the dishes.

She smiled as she heard Dicka say, "One thing at a time, and that done well, is a good plan. Let's not skip rope while *this* cake is in the oven."

Each little girl took her turn at stirring.

Flicka poured the batter into the pan, which Aunt Betty had cleaned. Dicka put the cake into the oven. Then the three girls sat down to watch the clock. At just the right minute Flicka took out the cake.

Aunt Betty showed them how to turn it over onto a plate.

This cake was a lovely yellow-and-brown color.

"It's perfectly baked!" Aunt Betty exclaimed.

After it cooled, she helped them frost it. Finally, Flicka, Ricka, and Dicka put small pieces of candied fruit all over the frosting.

When they were through, Dicka waved her apron happily because the cake was so beautiful.

Dicka waved her apron happily.

It is the most beautiful birthday present we ever made!" the girls said. Then they took the cake home.

When Father saw it, he said proudly, "Mother will love it. Let's hide it until tomorrow."

"Let's ask Mother to sleep late on her birthday," said Ricka. "Then we can take the cake up to her room."

In the morning the three little girls jumped out of bed and fixed a tray for Mother.

Father got the cake from its hiding place. Flicka made tea. Dicka got out a teacup. Ricka picked some pretty flowers.

The three little girls fixed a tray for Mother.

Now everything was ready.
Flicka carried the cake.

Dicka carried the tray with tea and cream and sugar on it.

Ricka carried her bunch of flowers.

When they reached Mother's room, they all began to sing:

Happy birthday to you,
Happy birthday to you,
Happy birthday, dear Mother,
Happy birthday to you!

Mother was waiting. "How nice!" she said.

"We wanted to surprise you," said Flicka. "We baked this cake because we know it is the kind you like best."

"And so it is," Mother said. "I love this cake, but I love my three little daughters even more."

"Happy birthday, dear Mother."